Ugly Dogs
and Slimy Frogs

Retold by Rose Impey

Illustrated by *Peter Bailey*

ORCHARD BOOKS

Other titles in this series:

Bad Boys and Naughty Girls

Greedy Guts and Belly Busters

If Wishes were Fishes

I Spy, Pancakes and Pies

Silly Sons and Dozy Daughters

ORCHARD BOOKS
96 Leonard Street, London EC2A 4XD
Orchard Books Australia
14 Mars Road, Lane Cove, NSW 2066
First published in Great Britain in 1999
First paperback publication 2000
Text © Rose Impey 1999
Illustrations © Peter Bailey 1999
The rights of Rose Impey to be identified as the author
and Peter Bailey as the illustrator of this work
have been asserted by them in accordance with the
Copyright, Designs and Patents Act, 1988.
A CIP catalogue record for this book is available
from the British Library.
1 86039 963 0 (hardback)
1 86039 964 9 (paperback)
1 3 5 7 9 10 8 6 4 2 (hardback)
1 3 5 7 9 10 8 6 4 2 (paperback)
Printed in Great Britain

★ CONTENTS ★

The Great Big Horrid Small-tooth Dog

One dark and stormy night a rich man was travelling home when he was set upon by thieves.

They pulled him off his horse and took all his money. They'd probably have killed him, but just then a huge dog came out of the darkness and chased the thieves away.

"Oh, thank you," said the man. "You've saved my life! I must give you a reward."

"I'm sure you'll think of something," said the dog, showing two rows of small, neat teeth.

The first thing the man thought of was his hen that laid golden eggs.

"I don't want that," said the dog, reading his mind.

The next thing the man thought of was his magic mirror. You only had to look into it to tell what someone was thinking.

"And I don't need that," said the dog.

Then, before
he could stop
himself, the
man thought
of his daughter.
She was his
greatest
treasure and the
dog knew it.

"Yes, that's
what I'd like,"
said the dog.
"I'll come
for her in a
week's time."

The man went home weighed down with grief. He couldn't bear to part with his daughter, and you can be sure she wasn't happy about it, either.

"Go and live with a horrid great dog?" she said. "I'm not doing that. You can't make me, Father."

But he could and he did. The man had no choice; he owed the dog his life.

When the dog came to fetch
the girl, she looked at him and
shuddered.

He had eyes as green as glass.
He had a long red tongue, lolling
out of his mouth. And all over
him was thick shaggy hair.

"Get up on my back," the dog growled, showing his small, neat teeth.

The poor girl did as she was told and the great big shaggy dog galloped for miles and miles until they came to his house.

It was a lovely house and had everything in it the girl could possibly want. But by the end of a month she looked quite ill with crying.

"Tell me what's wrong," growled the dog, but it wasn't an angry growl.

"I want to see my father," she sobbed. "I'm homesick."

"I'll take you home," said the
dog. "You can stay for three days.
But before you go, tell me what
you call me."

"Call you?" said the girl. "What
else would I call you, but a great
big horrid small-tooth dog."

"Well, if that's what you think," said the dog, "I won't take you."

And he went away, leaving her sobbing her heart out.

Another week went by, with the
dog trying to be kind. He gave
her plenty to eat, in fact anything
her heart desired. But the girl was
still crying.

At last he said, "All right, I will take you home, but tell me first, what do you call me?"

"Sweet-as-honey," said the girl, as quick as a flash. "That's what I call you."

Then she jumped up on his back
and he ran like the wind. When
they came to a stile the dog
stopped and said, "Tell me again
what you call me."

By now the
girl's head
was full of
thoughts of
home and
seeing her
father. She
looked at
the ugly
big dog and
shuddered.
"A great
big horrid
small-tooth
dog," she
said. "What
else would I
call you?"

The dog sighed. He didn't say a word, but he turned round and ran back to his house with the girl sobbing and crying.

Another week went by and the girl begged the dog to take her home.

When he said, "First, tell me what you call me", she had her answer ready: "Sweet-as-honey, of course."

Then off they went again, mile after mile, over the first stile and on till they came to a second stile. There the dog stopped. They were quite close to the girl's home now. She could see it in the distance. Surely she didn't need to pretend any more.

When the
great big
dog said,
"Just tell me
again what
you call
me", the
words
popped out
before she
could stop
them. "A
great big
horrid
small-tooth
dog. That's
what I call
you."

So the dog didn't jump the second stile. Oh, no, he turned round and took her right back home where they'd come from.

All the next week the dog tried to cheer her up, but nothing could make her smile. At last he said he would give her one more chance.

The girl didn't wait to be asked. "Sweet-as-honey, that's what I call you," she said.

"Jump up then," he growled, not at all angry this time.

Well, they almost flew there. Over the first stile, over the second stile. All the way she kept whispering "*Sweet-as-honey*" in his ear, just in case the dog changed his mind.

At last they reached the girl's house. She jumped down and ran up the steps. Her hand was already on the door-knocker.

Nothing could stop her now. But the dog called in a low, sad voice, "Before you go, tell me what you call me."

The girl almost laughed. She turned towards him and said, "You're a great big—" She was going to say *horrid*, but then she looked into the dog's sad eyes.

She thought of how kind he had been to her, and how hard he had tried to please her. She ran back down the steps and threw her arms round his neck.

"You're a great big… sweetheart," she said, hugging and kissing him. "Sweet-as-honey, that's what I call you."

Then the great big dog stood up on his great back legs and with one great big pull he tore off his dog's head. His shaggy coat fell away and there he stood – a tall, handsome, small-tooth prince.

Well, you can be sure the girl
was happy now. *Sweet-as-honey, my
own sugar plum, angel-cake.* Oh,
there was no end to the names she
called him after that.

She called him "sweet" and
broke the spell.
And everything afterwards
turned out well.

The Lassie and the Frog

Have you ever heard the story of the wee lassie who went to fetch water from the well and ended up a princess? Well, here it is.

There was once a poor widow and her daughter. The woman worked hard, terribly hard. And when she came home from her work she was often tired and bad-tempered.

The housework fell to her daughter and there was plenty of it. Even the water had to be fetched from the well which was a mile away.

One day the lassie set out for the well as usual, but on her way back — horror of horrors! — she broke the jug.

When her mother came home she was so angry she sent the lassie straight back to the well. And she gave her nothing but a sieve to collect the water in.

Well, that was a hopeless task and the lassie knew it. When she reached the well she was in despair. But she didn't dare go home again, so she sat and she sobbed her heart out.

Suddenly, out of the well, a frog
came jump–jump–jumping.

"What's the matter, my dearie?"
it croaked.

"Look at this," said the lassie, holding out the sieve. "My mother's sent me to fetch water in it. But no one can do that."

"I can tell you how to do it," said the frog. "But if I do, what will you give me?"

Well, the wee lassie was poor and hadn't much to offer.

"I'll give you my skipping rope," she said. "Or my glass beads. Or my best handkerchief."

"They're no use to me," said the frog.

But the lassie had nothing else to give.

So the frog said, "If you'll marry me, I'll tell you."

Marry a frog! He must be joking, she thought. But the lassie was at her wits' end, so she said, "Aye, all right, if only you'll help me."

So then the frog told her what
to do:

> "Fill it with moss
> And spread it with clay,
> Then you can carry
> The water away."

So that's just what the lassie did.

As soon as the clay dried she
filled the sieve and hurried home
as fast as she could without
spilling the water. She never even
looked back at the frog.

When her mother saw how clever the lassie had been, it put her in a much better mood. Until suppertime at least.

But when the two of them sat down to eat, there came a splish, splash, splosh sound outside the door. Then a croaking voice sang out:

"*Open the door, my hinny,*
my heart,
Open the door, my dearie.
Open the door, my own wee wife;
Remember the promise you
made me."

The lassie could hardly believe
her ears. Open the door to a
horrid frog? She would rather lock
and bolt it.

But when her mother heard all about the frog and how he'd helped her, she said, "A promise is a promise and must be kept."

So the lassie got up and let the slimy, slippery frog in. Slip, slap, slop, it went, slip, slap, slop, across the floor.

The frog waited by her chair.
Then it croaked:

"Give me some supper, my hinny,
my heart,
Give me some supper, my dearie.
Give me some supper, my own
wee wife;
Remember the promise you
made me."

"Share my supper with a nasty, slimy frog? I will not," said the lassie.

But her mother said, "Whisht! Lassies must keep their promises. Now, give the poor creature some supper."

So the lassie picked the frog up by its wet leg and put it on the table right beside her plate. And wasn't that enough to put her off her food?

But even now the frog wasn't happy. It started up again:

"Take me to bed, my hinny,
my heart,
Take me to bed, my dearie.
Take me to bed, my own wee wife;
Remember the promise you
made me."

Well, the lassie wouldn't do that. Share her bed with a cold, wet frog? No thank you! But her mother said, "Do what you promised, daughter. You made your bed and now you must lie in it."

So the poor lassie had to do it. She picked up the frog between two fingers and carried him up to bed.

But she wouldn't lie anywhere near him. She lay the whole night on the very edge of the bed, hardly daring to close her eyes.

When morning came the frog
had another task for her. Imagine
her surprise when this time he said:

*"Chop off my head, my hinny,
my heart,
Chop off my head, my dearie.
Chop off my head, my own wee wife;
Remember the promise
you made me."*

Oh no, the lassie wouldn't do *that*. He might be a cold, wet, slimy frog, but she couldn't bear to hurt him.

But the frog said it once, twice, three times and in the end the lassie had to go and fetch the axe.

She put the frog on the floor
and lifted the axe. Whoosh! One
chop and off flew his head. And
there in his place was a handsome
young prince.

He smiled at her and said,
"Thank you. You've saved me
at last."

Then he told her how a wicked
fairy had cast a spell on him.

Now the lassie had broken the
spell by doing everything he'd
asked. So, when he asked again if
she'd marry him, this time she was
all for it.

The two of them returned to his palace, got married and lived happily ever after.

His head flew off with one
swift CHOP!
This tale's finished.
Now I'll stop.

Transformations (where animals turn into human beings, usually a handsome prince or princess) are very common in folk and fairy tales.
The Small-Tooth Dog comes from the Midlands and is similar to *Beauty and the Beast.*
The Lassie and the Frog is a mixture of *The Frog Prince* and the Scottish story *The Well of the World's End.*

Here are some more stories
you might like to read:

About Transformations:

The Frog Prince *and* Beauty and the Beast
from *The Orchard Book of Fairy Tales*
by Rose Impey
(Orchard Books)

The Lemon Princess
from *The Orchard Book of Magical Tales*
by Margaret Mayo
(Orchard Books)

About Frogs:

The Big-Wide-Mouthed-Toad-Frog
from *The Big-Wide-Mouthed-Toad-Frog
        and Other Stories*
by Mary Medlicott
(Kingfisher)